DETECTIVE GURUNADAM: THE CASE FILES

APPALLA YAZNA SURYA SAI KIRAN

Contents

Preface

The world of detective fiction is one of mystery, intrigue, and suspense. It is a genre that has captivated readers for generations and continues to do so to this day. A detective novel is a unique form of storytelling, one that combines the thrill of a puzzle with the emotional depth of a character study.

This novel follows the story of Detective Gurunadam, a seasoned detective with a keen mind and a dedication to justice. He is faced with a series of challenging cases that test his skills and determination. From the gritty streets of Nayakpur to the high-society circles of the wealthy and powerful, Detective Gurunadam leaves no stone unturned in his quest to solve each case.

But Detective Gurunadam is more than just a detective, he is also a complex and fully-realized character, with his own struggles and personal demons. As he delves deeper into each case, he must also confront his own past and the choices he has made.

This novel is a page-turner that will keep you guessing until the very end. With its rich characters, intricate plots, and pulse-pounding action, it is sure to be a thrilling read for fans of detective fiction and crime novels.

CHAPTER ONE

DETECTIVE GURUNADAM

Detective Gurunadam was a man who had dedicated his life to finding the truth and seeking justice. He was born and raised in a small town, where his father was a well-respected detective. From a young age, Gurunadam knew that he wanted to follow in his father's footsteps and become a detective himself.

After completing his education, he joined the police academy and graduated at the top of his class. He quickly made a name for himself as a hardworking and dedicated detective. He had a keen eye for detail and was relentless in his pursuit of the truth.

It was this dedication that led him to take on the case of his father's murder. His father had been working on a high-profile case involving a powerful and corrupt businessman when he was brutally murdered in his home. The case was never solved, and the killer was never caught.

Gurunadam knew that his father's murder was not a random act of violence but was connected to the case he had been working on. He believed that the businessman was behind the murder, desperate to silence anyone who could expose his crimes.

He spent years investigating the case, facing obstacles and setbacks along the way. But he never gave up, determined to find the truth and bring his father's killer to justice. He poured over the evidence and interview transcripts and followed every lead no matter how small.

Through his hard work, he was able to prove the businessman guilty of the murder and bring him to trial. But even as the businessman was led away in handcuffs, Gurunadam knew that the fight was not over. He knew he had to stay vigilant and continue to gather evidence to ensure that the businessman stayed behind bars.

Gurunadam's dedication to finding the truth and bringing his father's killer to justice earned him the respect and admiration of his colleagues.

He became known as one of the most respected and feared detectives in the department. He had finally found closure and peace knowing that his father's death was avenged.

But his work was not only limited to his father's murder case, he was well known for his dedication and success in solving the most complex cases and bringing criminals to justice. He had a sense of justice which made him a fearless detective and a respected member of the community. He continued to serve as a detective, helping to bring criminals to justice and making the streets a safer place for everyone.

CHAPTER TWO

NAYAKPUR

The fictional Indian city of "Nayakpur" is a bustling metropolis located in the northern region of the country. Known for its rich history, Nayakpur is a melting pot of cultures and religions, with a diverse population of Hindus, Muslims, Sikhs, and Christians. The city is home to many famous historical landmarks, including the ancient "Nayak Fort," which dates back to the Mughal era and offers a stunning view of the city from its battlements.

The city is also known for its vibrant street life, with colorful bazaars selling everything from traditional handicrafts to modern electronics. The "Chowk Bazaar" is particularly famous for its street food, where one can enjoy a wide variety of delicacies from different parts of India.

Nayakpur is also a major center of education and culture. The city is home to several prestigious universities, including the "Nayakpur University," which is renowned for its faculties of literature, history, and engineering. The city is also home to several museums, art galleries, and theaters, making it a popular destination for art and culture enthusiasts.

Despite the rapid modernization, Nayakpur has managed to preserve its traditional charm and character, making it a fascinating destination for both tourists and residents alike.

CHAPTER THREE

Murder in the Family: The Unsolved Mystery of Detective Gurunadam's Father

Detective Gurunadam's father, also a detective, had been working on a high-profile case involving a powerful and corrupt businessman. The businessman was suspected of embezzlement, money laundering, and other white-collar crimes.

Gurunadam's father had been getting close to uncovering the truth and was about to present his findings to the district attorney when he was brutally murdered in his home. The case was never solved and the killer was never caught.

Gurunadam was devastated by his father's death and vowed to find the killer and bring them to justice. He dedicated his life to solving the case, pouring over the evidence and interview transcripts, and following every lead no matter how small.

As he dug deeper into the case, he began to suspect that his father's murder was not a random act of violence but was in fact connected to the case he had been working on. He believed that the businessman was behind the murder, desperate to silence anyone who could expose his crimes.

Gurunadam spent years investigating the case, facing obstacles and setbacks along the way. But he never gave up, determined to find the truth and bring his father's killer to justice.

Detective Gurunadam sat in his office, staring at the photo of his father on his desk. It had been three years since his father's murder, and

Gurunadam was no closer to finding the killer. He had devoted his life to solving the case, but every lead had led to a dead end.

One day, a break in the case finally came. A witness came forward with information about a man who had been seen near the scene of the murder on the night it occurred. Gurunadam quickly set out to track the man down, and after a long and difficult search, he finally found him.

The man, who went by the name of John, was a shady character with a criminal record a mile long. Gurunadam knew that he was the one he had been looking for, but he needed more evidence before he could make an arrest.

Gurunadam spent weeks gathering evidence and building a case against John. He interviewed witnesses, collected fingerprints, and pieced together a timeline of events. Finally, he had enough evidence to bring John to trial.

The trial was a long and grueling process, but in the end, the evidence was too strong to ignore. John was found guilty of murder and sent to prison for life.

But just as Gurunadam was about to close the case and finally have some closure, he received a surprise visit from John's lawyer. The lawyer revealed that John had been coerced into confessing to the murder by the real killer, a powerful and corrupt businessman who had been using John as a scapegoat to cover up his own crime.

Gurunadam was shocked and outraged. He knew that he had to bring the real killer to justice, no matter what it took. He spent months gathering evidence and building a case against the businessman, and in the end, he was able to prove his guilt beyond a doubt.

The businessman was arrested and brought to trial, and just as John had been, he was found guilty and sent to prison for life.

Gurunadam finally had closure, he had found his father's killer and brought him to justice. He knew that nothing could bring his father back, but at least he could rest easy knowing that the person who had taken his father's life was finally behind bars.

As the trial began, the businessman, who went by the name of Robert, used all of his resources and connections to try and clear his name. He hired the best lawyers money could buy and used his influence to sway public opinion in his favor.

Gurunadam knew that he had a tough fight ahead of him, but he was determined to see justice done. He worked tirelessly to present the evidence he had collected and to refute the defense's arguments.

The trial was long and grueling, but in the end, the evidence was too strong to ignore. The jury returned a guilty verdict, and Robert was sentenced to life in prison.

But even as Robert was led away in handcuffs, Gurunadam knew that the fight was not over. Robert had powerful friends in high places, and Gurunadam knew that they would stop at nothing to clear his name and secure his release.

Gurunadam knew that he had to stay vigilant and continue to gather evidence to ensure that Robert stayed behind bars. He worked tirelessly to build a case against Robert's associates and to expose any attempts at corruption or bribery.

Through his hard work, Gurunadam was able to keep Robert locked up and ensure that justice was done. He knew that he could never bring his father back, but he could at least make sure that his father's killer was held accountable for his actions.

Gurunadam's dedication to finding the truth and bringing his father's killer to justice earned him the respect and admiration of his colleagues, and he became known as one of the most respected and feared detectives in the department. He had finally found closure and peace knowing that his father's death was avenged.

CHAPTER FOUR

Breaking and Entering: The Case of the Master Burglars and Detective Gurunadam

In 2010, Detective Gurunadam was called to investigate a string of burglaries in a wealthy neighborhood. The burglaries had been occurring over the course of several months, and the police were struggling to find any leads.

Gurunadam immediately began to investigate the case, interviewing the victims and studying the crime scenes. He quickly realized that these burglaries were not the work of amateurs, but of a skilled and well-organized criminal gang.

Gurunadam knew that he would have to use all of his expertise and resources to track down the burglars and bring them to justice. He set up surveillance on known criminal hangouts and began to gather evidence.

As he delved deeper into the case, Gurunadam discovered that the burglars were using high-tech equipment and techniques to break into the houses. He also learned that they were targeting specific homes, stealing only valuable items and leaving behind anything that could not be easily sold.

Gurunadam knew that he was getting close to the truth, but he still needed more evidence to make an arrest. He decided to set up a sting operation to catch the burglars in the act. He and his team set up cameras and monitoring equipment in one of the houses and waited for the burglars to strike.

Their plan worked perfectly. The burglars broke into the house, and the police were able to arrest them before they could escape. The burglars were found to be a group of ex-cons who had been released from prison recently and were in need of money.

Thanks to Gurunadam's hard work and dedication, the burglars were brought to justice and the residents of the neighborhood could sleep safely once again. His reputation as an excellent detective was once again reinforced. He was a skilled and experienced detective who was always willing to go the extra mile to solve a case and bring criminals to justice.

As the years went by, Detective Gurunadam continued to take on some of the most challenging cases in the department. He was known for his sharp intellect and ability to think outside the box, which helped him to solve cases that had stumped other detectives.

One of his most notable cases occurred in 2015, when a wealthy businessman was found murdered in his office. The businessman had a reputation for being ruthless and had many enemies, which made the list of suspects long.

Gurunadam was put in charge of the case, and he immediately began to investigate. He interviewed the businessman's colleagues, employees, and family members, but none of them seemed to have a motive for murder.

As he delved deeper into the case, Gurunadam began to suspect that the murder was not a personal vendetta, but rather a well-planned and executed crime. He started to investigate the businessman's business deals and financial transactions and found that the businessman had been involved in money laundering and embezzlement.

Gurunadam knew that he was getting close to the truth, but he still needed more evidence to make an arrest. He decided to set up a sting operation, and with the help of his team, they were able to catch the real killer, who turned out to be one of the businessman's business partners who was trying to cover his tracks by eliminating the businessman.

The case was solved, and the killer was brought to justice, thanks to Gurunadam's relentless pursuit of the truth. His reputation as an excellent detective continued to grow, and he became a mentor to many of the younger detectives in the department.

Despite his success, Gurunadam never let fame get to his head. He remained humble and dedicated, always putting the needs of his cases and community before his own. He continued to serve as a detective, helping to make the streets safer for everyone and maintaining his reputation as one of the best detectives in the department.

CHAPTER FIVE

Killer in the Classroom: The Hunt for the Student Killer and Detective Gurunadam

The serial killer had a troubled past. Growing up in a broken home, he was subjected to physical and emotional abuse from a young age. This traumatic experience left him with deep psychological scars and a twisted worldview.

As he grew older, the killer became increasingly isolated and disconnected from society. He had difficulty forming relationships and found it hard to hold down a job. He turned to alcohol and drugs to numb the pain of his past, but it only made things worse.

His descent into madness began when he was fired from his last job, and he felt like the whole world was against him. He began to blame society for his problems and decided to take revenge on the people he felt were responsible for his misery: young, successful college students.

He began to stalk his victims, studying their routines and habits, before striking at the perfect moment. He was careful to leave no evidence behind and was able to evade capture for a long time.

The serial killer's killings were brutal and meticulously planned. He targeted college students, specifically those who were high-achievers and had bright futures ahead of them. He felt a twisted sense of jealousy and resentment towards these individuals, believing that they had been given an unfair advantage in life.

He would stalk his victims for weeks, studying their routines and habits, before striking at the perfect moment. He would lure them to secluded locations, such as abandoned buildings or parks, and then brutally attack them.

His victims were found with multiple stab wounds, and it was clear that the killer took sadistic pleasure in their suffering. He would often leave cryptic messages at the crime scenes, taunting the police and the city.

The killer was also known for mutilating the bodies of his victims, which caused immense shock and horror among the public. The police had a hard time identifying the victims as the killer would leave the bodies in a state that is hard to recognize.

As the body count rose, the city was gripped by fear and panic. Parents were afraid to let their children out of the house, and many students were too scared to attend classes. The killer had successfully instilled a sense of terror in the hearts of the people, and it seemed that no one was safe from his wrath.

The serial killer's first known killing was that of a college student named Emily. She was a bright and ambitious young woman, who was on the verge of graduating at the top of her class. She had a bright future ahead of her and had already received job offers from some of the top companies in the city.

One evening, Emily had stayed late at the library to finish a project. As she was leaving, the killer approached her, pretending to be lost and asking for directions. Emily, being a kind-hearted person, offered to help and walked with the killer.

The killer led her to an abandoned warehouse on the outskirts of the city. Inside, he overpowered her and brutally attacked her. He stabbed her multiple times and left her to die alone in the dark.

The police were alerted when Emily failed to return home that night. They searched for her and eventually found her body in the abandoned warehouse. The killer had left behind a message scrawled in blood on the wall, taunting the police and the city.

The news of Emily's death shook the city to its core. It was the first indication that there was a ruthless killer on the loose and that no one was safe. The city was plunged into a state of fear and panic as the police struggled to find the killer and bring him to justice.

The serial killer's second known killing was that of a college student named Ramu. He was a hardworking student who came from a working-class family. He was determined to succeed and make a better life for himself and his family.

Ramu was last seen leaving the campus library late one evening. The killer had been watching him for weeks, studying his habits and routines. He knew that Ramu often stayed late to study and that he would be alone and vulnerable.

The killer approached Ramu as he was walking home, pretending to be lost and asking for directions. Ramu, being a helpful person, offered to walk with the killer. The killer led him to a secluded park on the outskirts of the city.

Once they reached the park, the killer overpowered Ramu and brutally attacked him. He stabbed him multiple times and left him to die alone in the park.

The police were alerted when Ramu failed to return home that night. They searched for him and eventually found his body in the park. The killer had left behind a message scrawled in blood on a nearby tree, taunting the police and the city.

The news of Ramu's death was met with shock and outrage. It was clear that the killer was targeting vulnerable students and that no one was safe. The police stepped up their efforts to find the killer and bring him to justice, but he remained elusive.

The serial killer's third known killing was that of a college student named Eswari. She was the daughter of a wealthy and powerful businessman, who was known for his greed and drug addiction. Despite her privileged background, Eswari was a hardworking student who was in her final year of college at Sri Vydyananda College.

Eswari was last seen leaving a party late one night. The killer had been watching her for weeks, studying her habits and routines. He knew that she was a party-goer and that she would be alone and vulnerable.

The killer approached Eswari as she was walking home, pretending to be lost and asking for directions. Eswari, being a kind-hearted person, offered to walk with the killer. The killer led her to a secluded alleyway near her home.

Once they reached the alleyway, the killer overpowered Eswari and brutally attacked her. He stabbed her multiple times and left her to die alone in the alleyway.

The police were alerted when Eswari failed to return home that night. They searched for her and eventually found her body in the alleyway. The killer had left behind a message scrawled in blood on a nearby wall, taunting the police and the city.

The news of Edward's death was met with shock and outrage. It was clear that the killer was targeting vulnerable students regardless of their background and that no one was safe. The police stepped up their efforts to find the killer and bring him to justice, but he remained elusive.

Detective Gurunadam is on the trail of a ruthless serial killer who has been targeting college students. As the body count rises, Gurunadam becomes more determined to catch the killer and bring an end to the reign of terror.

The investigation leads Gurunadam down a twisted path, filled with false leads and dead ends. The killer always seems to be one step ahead, leading Gurunadam on a wild goose chase through the city.

As the pressure mounts, Gurunadam begins to suspect that the killer may be someone he knows, someone close to him. This suspicion is confirmed when he receives a cryptic message from the killer, taunting him and hinting at a personal connection.

Witnesses: The police interviewed witnesses who may have seen or interacted with the killer. They also canvassed the areas where the murders took place, looking for anyone who may have seen something suspicious.

Surveillance footage: The police reviewed surveillance footage from the areas where the murders took place, looking for anyone who matched the killer's description. They also checked footage from nearby businesses and homes to see if the killer was captured on camera.

Forensics: The police collected forensic evidence from the crime scenes, such as DNA and fingerprints. They also examined the victims' clothing and personal belongings for clues.

Profiling: The police worked with criminal psychologists to create a profile of the killer. This included information about the killer's personality, background, and motivations.

Public appeals: The police made public appeals for information, asking anyone with knowledge of the killings to come forward. They also offered a reward for information that led to the killer's capture.

Collaboration: The police worked closely with other law enforcement agencies and organizations to share information and resources. This included other local police departments, the FBI, and crime victims' advocacy groups.

Following up on leads: Police followed up on any leads that were received, whether it be from a witness, a tip, or a hunch. They also worked on connecting these leads to the previous crimes and identifying any patterns or similarities.

Utilizing technology: Police used the latest technology like facial recognition, DNA matching, and phone tracking to identify the killer, and also to track his movements to narrow the search.

Undercover operations: Police also considered undercover operations, where they would send an officer to try and gain the killer's trust and gather the information that could lead to his capture.

With this new information, Gurunadam is able to narrow down the list of suspects and eventually zero in on the killer. The final confrontation takes place in an abandoned warehouse, where Gurunadam and the killer engage in a brutal fight.

In the end, Gurunadam is able to apprehend the killer, but not before the killer reveals that he has an accomplice still at large.

NOTE: It is hinted that this accomplice may be the true mastermind behind the killings and potentially the main antagonist for a sequel.

CHAPTER SIX

The Diagn of Deception: Detective Gurunadam and his Sister Uncover the Medical Mafia

Detective Gurunadam had always been a loner, dedicating his life to solving crimes and seeking justice. But he had one family member who cared deeply for him - his older sister Gayatri. Gayatri was a successful doctor and the two of them had always been close. However, their relationship had been strained for many years due to a tragic event in their past.

When Gurunadam and Gayatri were children, their mother was killed in a car accident. Gayatri, who was 14 at the time, was the only one who survived the crash. She was left with severe injuries and was in a coma for several weeks. When she woke up, she was told that her mother had died. The trauma of the accident and the loss of her mother had left Gayatri with deep emotional scars.

Gurunadam, who was only 8 at the time, had been deeply affected by the loss of his mother and the trauma of watching his sister suffer. He had grown up feeling guilty for not being able to save his family and had turned to solving crimes as a way to cope with his feelings of helplessness. Gayatri, on the other hand, had turned to her medical career as a way to make sense of her own trauma and to help others.

The two siblings had grown apart over the years, with Gayatri focusing on her career as a doctor and Gurunadam dedicating himself to solving crimes. They had not seen each other in many years and had not spoken much. Gayatri had struggled to understand her brother's obsession with solving crimes and had grown angry with him for not being able to move on from the past.

However, when a string of murders occurred in the medical community, both Gurunadam and Gayatri were pulled into the investigation. As they worked together to solve the case, they were forced to confront their past and the pain that had driven them apart. They began to understand each other's struggles and to heal the wounds that had separated them for so long.

As Gurunadam and Gayatri began to investigate the murders in the medical community, they quickly realized that these were not random killings. The victims all had connections to the Indian medical mafia, a powerful and corrupt group that controlled much of the country's healthcare system.

The first victim was a prominent surgeon who had refused to take bribes from the mafia to perform unnecessary surgeries. The second victim was a nurse who had witnessed a bribe being paid to a doctor and had threatened to report it. The third victim was a pharmacist who had refused to distribute counterfeit drugs to hospitals.

Their investigation leads them to the fourth victim, a young woman named Lavanya who had been receiving treatment for cancer. She had been getting better, but suddenly her condition took a turn for the worse and she died. Gurunadam and his sister were suspicious and decided to investigate her death. They found out that the medical mafia had given her the wrong treatment, which caused her death.

As they dug deeper into the case, Gurunadam and Gayatri discovered that the Indian medical mafia had infiltrated every aspect of the healthcare system, from hospitals and clinics to pharmaceutical companies and government agencies. They were using their power and influence to control the distribution of medical supplies and drugs, extort money from doctors and hospitals, and silence anyone who dared to speak out against them.

Gurunadam and Gayatri soon found themselves in a dangerous situation as they were getting closer to finding the truth. They received death threats, their offices were ransacked, and they were followed by unknown people. They knew that the Indian medical mafia would stop at nothing to keep their illegal activities hidden, and they knew that they were in grave danger.

But the two siblings were determined to bring the killers to justice and to expose the corruption that was plaguing the healthcare system. They worked tirelessly, piecing together clues and gathering evidence, and they were finally able to identify the key players in the mafia.

With the help of the police, they were able to arrest the suspects and bring them to trial. They also used the evidence they had gathered to expose the corruption in the healthcare system and to push for reforms that would help to prevent similar crimes in the future.

In the end, their shared tragedy brought them back together, and they were able to find closure and peace together. The case had been solved and both of them had found a new purpose and a renewed sense of hope for the future.

CHAPTER SEVEN

Revenge Redux: Detective Gurunadam's Past Enemies Strike Again

In 2016, Detective Gurunadam was on his way home from work when he was suddenly attacked on the street. He was beaten and left unconscious, and when he awoke in the hospital, he had no memory of the attack.

Gurunadam was determined to find out who had attacked him and why. He began to investigate, but the case seemed to have no leads. He was frustrated and couldn't understand why someone would want to hurt him.

As he delved deeper into the case, he started to notice similarities with two of his past cases, the one he solved in 2010 and 2015. He realized that the attackers could be someone connected to those cases.

He decided to review those cases again, and it was then that he discovered that the attackers were the brothers of the burglars he had arrested in 2010 and the business partner he had put in jail in 2015. They had been released from prison recently and were seeking revenge on Gurunadam for putting their family members behind bars.

Gurunadam knew he had to act fast before they could harm him or anyone else.

Interviews with witnesses: They spoke to anyone who saw the attack, in order to gather information about the attackers and their movements.

Surveillance footage: They reviewed footage from security cameras in the area where the attack took place, in order to see if they could identify the attackers or their vehicle.

Phone records: They analyzed Gurunadam's phone records, in order to see if he had any recent calls or texts from the attackers.

Previous cases: They went through Gurunadam's previous cases, looking for any suspects who may have had a grudge against him.

Psychological profile of the attackers: They worked with a criminal profiler to build a psychological profile of the attackers, in order to understand their motivations and predict their behavior.

Tracking the attackers' movements: They used eyewitness accounts, surveillance footage, and other leads to track the attackers' movements and try to identify them.

Fingerprint and DNA analysis: They analyzed any fingerprints or DNA left behind by the attackers at the crime scene to identify them.

Reviewing any threats or warnings received by Gurunadam or his department in the past.

Checking for any security breaches in the Gurunadam's personal or professional life.

He gathered evidence and got a warrant to arrest them. With the help of his team, he was able to track them down and bring them to justice.

The attackers were found guilty of attempted murder and were sentenced to life in prison. Gurunadam's determination and dedication to finding the truth once again led to the capture of dangerous criminals.

Despite being attacked, Gurunadam's spirit was unbroken and he continued to serve as a detective with even more vigor. He knew that being a detective was not only about solving cases but also about keeping the community safe, and he was determined to do just that.

CHAPTER EIGHT

Vanished: Detective Gurunadam's Search for the Gone Girl

After the attackers were captured and brought to justice, Detective Gurunadam was hailed as a hero by the community. His colleagues and superiors praised him for his determination and dedication to solving the case, despite being the victim himself.

However, the attack had taken a toll on him. He was left with physical and emotional scars, and he struggled to come to terms with what had happened. He was plagued by nightmares and flashbacks of the attack, and he couldn't shake off the feeling of vulnerability.

Gurunadam's family and friends noticed the changes in him and were worried about his well-being. They encouraged him to seek counseling, and he eventually opened up about his feelings to a therapist. With the help of therapy, he was able to work through his trauma and come to terms with what had happened.

Despite his personal struggles, Gurunadam never let them affect his work. He was determined to continue serving as a detective and protecting the community. However, he made a conscious effort to prioritize his mental health and take time off when he needed it.

One day, a new case came across his desk. A young girl had gone missing, and her parents were desperate to find her. Gurunadam took the case, and it quickly became personal for him. He was determined to find the girl and bring her home safely, and he wouldn't rest until the case was solved.

The case of the missing young girl quickly became the top priority for Detective Gurunadam and his team. They worked tirelessly, following leads and interviewing witnesses. As they delved deeper into the case, they discovered that the girl had been kidnapped by a man who had been stalking her for months.

Gurunadam and his team worked around the clock, analyzing evidence and tracking down leads.

Interviews with family and friends: They spoke to the girl's family and friends, in order to gather information about her habits, routines, and possible whereabouts.

Surveillance footage: They reviewed footage from security cameras in the area where the girl was last seen, in order to see if they could identify any potential suspects or witnesses.

Phone records: They analyzed the girl's phone records, in order to see if she had any recent calls or texts that could provide clues about her whereabouts.

Social media activity: They reviewed the girl's social media accounts, in order to see if she had posted any suspicious activity or messages.

Psychological profile of the girl: They worked with a criminal profiler to build a psychological profile of the girl, in order to understand her behavior and predict her movements.

Tracking the girl's movements: They used eyewitness accounts, surveillance footage, and other leads to track the girl's movements and try to identify her whereabouts.

Fingerprint and DNA analysis: They analyzed any fingerprints or DNA found at the location of the girl's disappearance to identify any suspects.

Reviewing any past cases of a missing person in the area and looking for any similarities.

Checking for any security breaches in the girl's personal or professional life.

They were determined to find the girl and bring her home safely. As the days passed, the community grew more and more worried about her whereabouts. They held vigils and prayed for her safe return.

Finally, after a week of intense searching, a break in the case came. A witness reported seeing the kidnapper's car parked outside a remote cabin in the woods. Gurunadam and his team immediately rushed to the cabin, and after a tense standoff, the kidnapper was apprehended and the girl was found unharmed.

The community was overjoyed at the news of the girl's safe return, and they thanked Detective Gurunadam and his team for their tireless efforts.

The girl's parents were eternally grateful and they thanked Gurunadam and his team for bringing their daughter back home.

Gurunadam, who had felt a personal connection to the case, was relieved that the girl was safe. He knew that being a detective was not just about solving cases, but also about being there for the victims and their families, and making a difference in the community. He felt proud of the work he and his team had done, and he knew that he would continue to serve and protect the community to the best of his abilities.

The kidnapper was charged with several serious crimes and was sentenced to life in prison. Gurunadam felt a sense of satisfaction knowing that the man responsible for the girl's abduction would never be able to hurt anyone again.

As Gurunadam closed the case, he couldn't help but feel a sense of closure. He realized that he was stronger than he had ever thought and that he could overcome any obstacle thrown his way. He was proud of the work he had done and the lives he had helped to save. He knew that being a detective was not only about solving cases but also about making a difference in the community, and he was determined to continue doing just that.

CHAPTER NINE

Murder on the Rails: Detective Gurunadam's Vacation Derails into a Deadly Mystery

Detective Gurunadam was looking forward to a much-needed vacation, but his plans were sidetracked when he was called to investigate a murder on board a luxurious train. The victim was a wealthy businessman, and all evidence points to a fellow passenger as the killer.

As Gurunadam boarded the train, he couldn't help but feel a sense of unease. The luxurious train was filled with wealthy and powerful people, and he knew that any one of them could be the killer.

As he walked through the train, he came across the body of the victim, who had been brutally murdered in his cabin. The room was in disarray, and it was clear that there had been a struggle. Gurunadam immediately knew that this was not going to be an easy case.

He started to investigate the other passengers and discovered that each one of them had a motive for the murder. The businessman had made many enemies throughout his career, and many of them were on the train.

Detective Gurunadam: Excuse me, ma'am. I'm Detective Gurunadam and I'm investigating a murder that occurred on this train. Can I ask you a few questions?

Innocent Fellow Passenger: Of course, Detective. I'll do whatever I can to help.

Detective Gurunadam: Can you tell me where you were and what you were doing on the night of the murder?

Innocent Fellow Passenger: I was in my cabin, reading a book. I didn't leave until the next morning.

Detective Gurunadam: Did you hear or see anything unusual that night?

Innocent Fellow Passenger: No, nothing at all. I was so engrossed in my book that I didn't even hear the commotion when the murder was discovered.

Detective Gurunadam: Do you know the victim or have any motive for wanting to harm them?

Innocent Fellow Passenger: No, I don't know the victim and I have no motive to harm them. I'm just an innocent passenger on this train.

Detective Gurunadam: All right, thank you for your cooperation. If you think of anything else, please let me know.

Innocent Fellow Passenger: Of course, Detective. I hope you find the person responsible for this terrible crime.

Gurunadam's investigation took him through the different cars of the train.

Detective Gurunadam: Good evening, Mr. Smith. I'm Detective Gurunadam and I'm investigating a murder that occurred on this train. Can I ask you a few questions?

Wealthy Socialite: Of course, Detective. I'll do whatever I can to help.

Detective Gurunadam: Can you tell me where you were and what you were doing on the night of the murder?

Wealthy Socialite: I was in my cabin, enjoying a glass of scotch and catching up on some work. I didn't leave until the next morning.

Detective Gurunadam: I see. And do you know the victim or have any motive for wanting to harm them?

Wealthy Socialite: No, I don't know the victim and I have no motive to harm them. I am a wealthy socialite and I have no need to resort to such actions.

Detective Gurunadam: I apologize, Mr. Smith, I had to ask. Your social status and wealth make you a prime suspect in this kind of case.

Wealthy Socialite: I understand, Detective. I am aware of the prejudices that come with my social status. But I assure you, I had nothing to do with this murder.

Detective Gurunadam: Alright, thank you for your cooperation. I will look into other leads.

Wealthy Socialite: Of course, Detective. I hope you find the person responsible for this terrible crime.

Detective Gurunadam: Good evening, sir. I'm Detective Gurunadam and I'm investigating a murder that occurred on this train. Can I ask you a few questions?

Jilted Lover: Yes, of course. I'll do whatever I can to help.

Detective Gurunadam: Can you tell me where you were and what you were doing on the night of the murder?

Jilted Lover: I was in my cabin, trying to get some sleep. I had just been through a rough break-up with my girlfriend and it was hard to close my eyes.

Detective Gurunadam: I see. And do you know the victim or have any motive for wanting to harm them?

Jilted Lover: No, I don't know the victim. I had no reason to harm anyone, especially after what I had just been through with my ex-girlfriend.

Detective Gurunadam: I apologize, sir, but as you know, jilted lovers are often prime suspects in these kinds of cases.

Jilted Lover: I understand, Detective. I know how it looks, but I swear I had nothing to do with this murder. I was just trying to move on with my life.

Detective Gurunadam: All right, thank you for your cooperation. I will look into other leads.

Jilted Lover: Of course, Detective. I hope you find the person responsible for this terrible crime.

Detective Gurunadam: Good evening, sir. I'm Detective Gurunadam and I'm investigating a murder that occurred on this train. Can I ask you a few questions?

Rival Businessman: Yes, of course. I'll do whatever I can to help.

Detective Gurunadam: Can you tell me where you were and what you were doing on the night of the murder?

Rival Businessman: I was in my cabin, working on some paperwork for my company. I had a lot of meetings and deals to attend to.

Detective Gurunadam: I see. And do you know the victim or have any motive for wanting to harm them?

Rival Businessman: No, I don't know the victim. I had no reason to harm anyone.

Detective Gurunadam: I apologize, sir, but as you know, rival businessman are often prime suspects in these kinds of cases.

Rival Businessman: I understand, Detective. I know how it looks, but I swear I had nothing to do with this murder. I was just trying to run my business and make a living.

Detective Gurunadam: Alright, thank you for your cooperation. I will look into other leads.

Rival Businessman: Of course, Detective. I hope you find the person responsible for this terrible crime.

where he met a variety of characters, including a wealthy socialite, a jilted lover, and even a rival businessman. Each of them had a reason to want the victim dead, but Gurunadam could not find any solid evidence to link any of them to the murder.

As the train chugged along its route, Gurunadam was running out of time. He knew that the killer could strike again at any moment, and he had to find the real killer before they did.

Just as he was about to give up hope, Gurunadam received a tip from an unlikely source. The train's conductor had seen something suspicious on the night of the murder, and Gurunadam knew that this could be the break he had been looking for.

The train conductor, Mr. Patel, saw a few things on the night of the murder that may be relevant to the investigation. He reported seeing the victim, a young woman, sitting alone in the dining car around 8 PM. He also saw a man in a suit, who he later identified as the rival businessman, sitting across from her. The victim appeared to be upset and the businessman appeared to be trying to console her.

Mr. Patel also saw a jilted lover, who he recognized as a regular passenger, walking past the dining car several times throughout the evening. The man appeared to be agitated and was muttering to himself.

Finally, Mr. Patel reported that around midnight, he saw the victim's cabin door open and a man in a hooded sweatshirt slip out. He couldn't see the man's face, but he did notice that he was carrying a small bag.

When the train reached the next station and the police were notified, Mr. Patel immediately reported what he had seen to the investigating officers.

With the conductor's help, Gurunadam was able to piece together the events of the night.

As the investigation progresses, Detective Gurunadam begins to focus on a 17-year-old boy named Raj, who was a fellow passenger on the train. Raj had been traveling alone and was seen by multiple witnesses, including the train conductor, in the vicinity of the victim's cabin around the time of the murder.

Despite being young, Raj was a tech-savvy individual who has been able to manipulate the security camera footage to hide his presence. Gurunadam was able to track Raj down and interrogate him. The boy initially denied any involvement in the murder, but with the evidence that Gurunadam had gathered, Raj broke down and confessed to the crime.

It turns out that Raj had a grudge against the victim, who had rejected his advances. In a fit of rage, he had killed her and then tried to cover his tracks by manipulating the security footage. Despite his youth, Raj was charged with murder and faced trial for his crime.

The revelation that the unlikely source of the murder was a 17-year-old boy came as a shock to the other passengers and the public. It also served as a reminder of the dangers of underestimating anyone and the importance of a thorough investigation.

Gurunadam's vacation may have been sidetracked, but he was able to solve the murder and bring the killer to justice. But the case left him with a bitter taste, and he couldn't shake off the feeling that the killer was just one of many on the train. A reminder that even in the most luxurious surroundings, evil lurks.

CHAPTER TEN

The Haunting of Hillcrest Manor: Detective Gurunadam's Ghostly Investigation

In Hillcrest Manor, the owners and staff reported a variety of paranormal activities. Some of the occurrences include:

Strange noises: People heard unexplained footsteps, doors slamming shut, and other sounds coming from various parts of the mansion.

Ghostly apparitions: Several people reported seeing ghostly figures throughout the mansion. Some of the most commonly seen figures were believed to be previous occupants of the mansion who had died under mysterious circumstances.

Unusual temperature changes: Some areas of the mansion would suddenly become very cold, even in warm weather.

Objects moving on their own: Staff reported that objects, such as vases and picture frames, would move around the mansion without any explanation.

Electronic equipment malfunctioning: Many of the electronic devices in the mansion, such as lights and televisions, would turn on and off by themselves.

Inexplicable smells: Some people reported smelling strange odors, such as perfumes or cigars, that seemed to come out of nowhere.

These paranormal activities in the manor made the owners and staff worried and scared, it was Detective Gurunadam's job to uncover the truth and put the spirits to rest.

Detective Gurunadam was called to investigate a series of strange occurrences at a local mansion. The owners had reported hearing strange noises, seeing ghostly apparitions, and experiencing other inexplicable phenomena.

Gurunadam was skeptical at first, but as he began to investigate, he found that there was more to the case than he had initially thought. He interviewed the owners and the staff, whom all reported similar experiences. He also found that several previous occupants of the mansion had reported similar occurrences.

Detective Gurunadam interviewed the owner of Hillcrest Manor, Mr. James, and several of the staff members to gather more information about the strange occurrences happening in the mansion.

Mr. James reported that the mansion had been in his family for generations and that they had always heard stories of ghostly activity. He said that the activity had become more intense in recent months, and that's why he decided to call in a detective.

The staff members reported similar experiences, such as hearing strange noises and seeing ghostly apparitions. Some of them even claimed to have seen objects move on their own or to have had an electronic equipment malfunction.

One of the maids reported that she had seen a ghostly figure of a woman who appeared to be wearing a Victorian dress. She said that the woman seemed to be searching for something and that she had felt a cold breeze before the figure disappeared.

Another staff member, a gardener, claimed that he had seen a ghostly figure of a man in the garden who appeared to be searching for something as well. He said that the man had disappeared when he went to approach him.

Detective Gurunadam listened carefully to the reports and took note of all the details provided by the owner and the staff, he knew that solving the case would be a challenge but he was determined to get to the bottom of it.

As he delved deeper into the case, Gurunadam discovered that the mansion had a dark history. It had been built on an ancient burial ground, and several of the previous occupants had died under mysterious circumstances.

Gurunadam knew that he needed to unravel the mystery of the mansion to put the owners' minds at ease. He began to investigate the history of the mansion, and as he did so, he began to uncover a web of secrets and lies.

As Detective Gurunadam dug deeper into the case, he discovered that Hillcrest Manor had a dark history. He learned that the mansion was built in the 1800s by a wealthy businessman who had made his fortune in the shipping industry. However, the businessman had a secret past that involved illegal activities such as smuggling and extortion.

The businessman had used the mansion as a base of operations for his illegal activities, and it was said that he had hidden his ill-gotten gains in the walls and floors of the mansion. It was also rumored that he had imprisoned and even killed those who had crossed him.

Over the years, several people had attempted to search for hidden treasures and uncover the dark secrets of the mansion, but none had been successful. It was said that the businessman had placed curses and booby traps to protect his secrets and that those who dared to search for them would meet with misfortune.

As Detective Gurunadam delved deeper into the case, he realized that the strange occurrences in Hillcrest Manor might be connected to the dark history of the mansion. He began to suspect that the ghostly figures seen by the staff members were the spirits of those who had been wronged by the businessman and were now seeking justice.

Determined to uncover the truth and put the spirits to rest, Detective Gurunadam continued his investigation, knowing that the answers he was looking for lay hidden deep within the walls of Hillcrest Manor.

As the night fell, Gurunadam decided to explore the mansion on his own. He knew that the truth he was searching for would not reveal itself easily, and he was ready to face whatever lay ahead.

As he moved through the dark corridors, Gurunadam began to feel an overwhelming sense of dread. He heard whispers in the shadows, and the temperature dropped significantly. Suddenly, he heard a loud bang from one of the rooms, and he knew that he was not alone in the mansion.

Gurunadam cautiously opened the door to find a room that seemed to be in a state of disarray. Furniture was overturned, and there were signs of a struggle. Suddenly, he saw a ghostly figure appear in front of him. It was a woman dressed in old-fashioned clothing, and she seemed to be pointing at something in the corner of the room.

Gurunadam followed her gaze and discovered a hidden door. He opened it and found a secret room that was filled with documents and artifacts that revealed the dark secrets of the mansion. He finally realized that the ghostly figures were not trying to harm him, but were trying to lead him to the truth.

With the truth uncovered, Gurunadam knew that he had to put the spirits of Hillcrest Manor to rest. He returned to the room and spoke to the ghostly woman, apologizing for the wrongs that had been done to her and her family by the wealthy businessman who had built the mansion.

As he left the mansion, Gurunadam felt a sense of peace wash over him. He knew that the spirits of Hillcrest Manor had finally found the closure they had been seeking and that the mansion would no longer be haunted by their presence.

CHAPTER ELEVEN

The Reunited Sleuths: Detective Gurunadam and Yugandhar's Joint Investigation

Detective Yugandhar, an old friend of Detective Gurunadam, is called to investigate a murder at a hotel. Detective Gurunadam was on a routine case when he received a call from an old friend, Detective Yugandhan. They had worked together on many cases before, and Gurunadam was excited to hear from him again. Yugandhan explained that he was in town investigating a murder at a local hotel, and he needed Gurunadam's expertise.

Gurunadam quickly made his way to the hotel, where he was greeted by Yugandhan and his assistant, Raju. The three of them quickly got to work, going over the evidence and interviewing witnesses. They discovered that the murder was committed by a pair of twin suspects.

They began by interviewing the staff and witnesses to gather any information they could about the suspects and possible motives. The staff reported that they had seen two men, identical twins, acting suspiciously in the hotel lobby the night before the murder. They also reported that a wealthy businessman had been staying in the hotel at the time and had been seen arguing with the twins.

The detectives decided to question the businessman next. He initially denied any involvement in the murder but eventually confessed that he had been in a business dispute with the twin suspects and had confronted them the night before. He claimed that he had left the hotel after the argument and had no knowledge of the murder.

As the detectives continued their investigation, they collected evidence from the crime scene, including fingerprints and DNA samples. They also found a key piece of evidence in the form of a surveillance video that showed the twin suspects entering and leaving the victim's room on the night of the murder.

Despite the businessman's alibi, the detectives were still suspicious of him. They decided to question him further and search his hotel room for any additional evidence. They found a gun hidden in his luggage and arrested him for the murder.

The detectives and Raju spent the next few days piecing together the evidence and interviewing the twin suspects. They were able to gather enough evidence to build a strong case against the businessman, who was eventually convicted of the murder.

The case was solved thanks to the hard work and dedication of Detective Gurunadam, Detective Yugandhar, and Assistant Raju. They were able to bring justice to the victim's family and put a dangerous killer behind bars.

CHAPTER TWELVE

Haunted Past: Detective Gurunadam's Unsolved Crime

Detective Gurunadam has always been known for his exceptional solving skills and quick thinking. However, there is one case that has haunted him for years - the unsolved murder of a young woman named Sarah.

Sarah was a young woman from Gurunadam's hometown, and her brutal murder shook the community to its core. Despite his best efforts, Gurunadam was never able to bring her killer to justice.

Gurunadam had worked tirelessly on the case, but despite his best efforts, the killer was never caught. The case had taken a toll on him and he couldn't shake off the feeling of failure. He often found himself thinking about Sarah and the injustice that was done to her.

As fate would have it, a new lead emerged in the case many years later. A witness came forward with new information that could potentially crack the case wide open. Gurunadam jumped at the opportunity to finally bring closure to Sarah's murder and put the killer behind bars.

As he delved deeper into the case, he realized that there were many similarities to the original investigation. He soon discovered that the killer was someone close to Sarah and had been hiding in plain sight all along.

Gurunadam worked tirelessly to piece together the evidence and build a case against the killer. But as he got closer to the truth, he began to experience strange and terrifying occurrences. He would receive strange phone calls in the middle of the night, and he would see ghostly apparitions of Sarah everywhere he went.

Despite the eerie occurrences, Gurunadam refused to be deterred. He knew that it was his duty to solve the case and bring the killer to justice.

As he began to retrace the steps of the investigation, he found himself revisiting all the people who had been close to Sarah, including her family members and friends. He also interviewed new witnesses who had come forward with information that had not been available at the time of the murder.

Detective Gurunadam sat across from Sarah's mother, Mrs. Johnson, in the small, dimly lit interrogation room. He had been working on Sarah's case for months, but had hit a dead end until now.

"Mrs. Johnson, I understand this must be difficult for you, but I need to ask you some questions about your daughter," Detective Gurunadam began gently.

Mrs. Johnson nodded, her eyes red from crying. "I'll do whatever it takes to find out who did this to my little girl," she said, her voice shaking.

Detective Gurunadam pulled out a file from his briefcase and flipped through the pages. "We've received new evidence in the case that suggests that Sarah may have known her attacker. Can you think of anyone she may have had a disagreement with or any enemies she may have had?"

Mrs. Johnson thought for a moment before shaking her head. "Sarah was a good girl, she didn't have any enemies that I know of. She was always so kind to everyone."

Detective Gurunadam leaned forward, his eyes intense. "Mrs. Johnson, I need you to think hard. Is there anyone who may have had a grudge against Sarah or your family? Anyone who may have wanted to hurt her?"

Mrs. Johnson's face paled as she thought back to a few months before Sarah's death. "There was one person," she said, her voice barely audible. "He was an old friend of my husband's. They had a falling out over a business deal and he's been angry with us ever since."

Detective Gurunadam's heart raced. This was the break in the case he had been hoping for. "Can you give me his name and contact information?"

Mrs. Johnson nodded, tears streaming down her face. "His name is John Smith. I can give you his address and phone number."

Detective Gurunadam thanked Mrs. Johnson and quickly left the room. He knew he had to act fast to bring Sarah's killer to justice. As he walked out of the police station, he couldn't shake the feeling of unease. He had a hunch that this case was not going to be as simple as it seemed.

Detective Gurunadam sat across from John Smith, Sarah's father's old friend, in the dimly lit interrogation room. "Mr. Smith, can you tell me about your relationship with Sarah's father and your involvement in their lives?" Gurunadam asked, his pen poised over his notepad.

John shifted in his seat, clearly uncomfortable. "I've known Sarah's father for many years. We went to college together and have been friends ever since. I haven't seen much of him in recent years, but I always kept tabs on him and his family through mutual friends."

Gurunadam's eyes narrowed. "And what about your relationship with Sarah? Did you ever have any contact with her?"

John hesitated before answering. "I may have spoken to her on the phone a few times, but I never met her in person. I knew she was going through a tough time, and I wanted to be there for her if she needed someone to talk to."

Gurunadam scribbled notes onto his pad, his mind racing. "And where were you on the night of Sarah's murder?"

"I was at home," John replied quickly. "I have witnesses and alibis to prove it."

Gurunadam studied John for a moment before nodding. "Alright, thank you for your time, Mr. Smith. I'll be in touch if I have any more questions." As John left the room, Gurunadam couldn't shake off the feeling that there was more to this man's story than he was letting on. He made a note to dig deeper into John's alibis and background as he continued his investigation into Sarah's murder.

Gurunadam knew that this case would be his toughest yet, but he was determined to see it through to the end. He worked tirelessly, sifting through evidence and interviewing witnesses. He knew that he was getting closer to the truth, but he also knew that time was running out.

Detective Gurunadam sat across from Sarah's father, John, in the small, sparsely furnished living room of their modest home. John's eyes were red-rimmed and puffy, and his hands trembled as he clutched a photo of Sarah.

"Mr. Smith, I know this is difficult for you, but I need to ask you some questions about Sarah's case," Detective Gurunadam began softly.

John nodded, his voice barely above a whisper as he spoke. "I'll do anything to help find out what happened to my little girl."

Detective Gurunadam pulled out his notebook and pen, ready to take notes. "Can you tell me about Sarah's relationships? Did she have any conflicts with anyone? Any ex-boyfriends or enemies?"

John shook his head. "No, Sarah was a good girl. She was popular in school and had a lot of friends. She didn't have any enemies that I know of. She was dating a boy named Tim, but they broke up a few months ago and it was amicable. They were still friends."

"Did Sarah have any plans or mention anything unusual before she went missing?"

John thought for a moment. "No, she didn't. She was just looking forward to her graduation and starting college in the fall. She had a part-time job at the mall and was saving up for a car."

Can you tell me about your friend John Smith?

Sarah's father looked down at his hands, which were clasped tightly in his lap. "John was my best friend," he said quietly. "We grew up together, went to school together, and stayed close even after we graduated. He's always been there for me and my family, through good times and bad."

Detective Gurunadham leaned forward, resting his arms on the table. "Can you tell me what John was doing on the night of Sarah's murder?"

Mr. Johnson shook his head. "I don't know. We weren't in touch that night. I didn't even know she had been killed until the next day. John was just as shocked as I was when he heard the news."

Detective Gurunadam made some notes in his notebook. "Can you think of anyone who may have had the motive to hurt Sarah? Anyone who may have wanted to harm her?"

John shook his head again. "No, I can't. Everyone loved Sarah. I don't understand how this could have happened."

Detective Gurunadam placed a hand on John's shoulder. "We're going to do everything we can to find out what happened to Sarah. We'll leave no stone unturned. I'll keep you updated on any developments."

John nodded, his voice choked with emotion. "Thank you, Detective. I just want my little girl back."

Detective Gurunadham sat back in his chair, studying Mr. Johnson's face. He could see the pain and grief etched there, and he knew that it was genuine. "I understand," he said. "I'll be in touch if I need anything else. Thank you for your time."

As Detective Gurunadham left the interview room, he couldn't help but feel a sense of unease. He had a feeling that John Smith was hiding something, but without any concrete evidence, there was nothing he could do. He promised himself that he would keep digging, for Sarah's sake, and for the sake of her family.

Detective Gurunadham sat across from Sarah's older sister, Emily, in the small, stuffy room. Emily's eyes were red and swollen from crying, and she clutched a tissue tightly in her hand.

"Emily, I know this is difficult for you, but I need to ask you some questions about your sister Sarah," Gurunadham said gently.

Emily nodded, wiping away a tear. "I'll do whatever I can to help find out who did this to her," she said, her voice shaking.

"Can you tell me about Sarah's relationship with her father and his friend, John Smith?" Gurunadham asked.

"John has been a family friend for as long as I can remember. He's always been like an uncle to us. Sarah was close to him, but I don't think they were particularly close in the months leading up to her death," Emily said.

"Did you notice any changes in Sarah's behavior or attitude recently?" Gurunadham pressed.

"No, not really. She seemed the same as always. She was happy and full of life," Emily replied.

"And what about your father? Was there any tension between him and Sarah?"

"No, not at all. They had a great relationship. My father loved Sarah more than anything," Emily said, her voice breaking.

Gurunadham nodded and made some notes in his notebook. "Thank you, Emily. I know this is hard for you, but your information is very helpful. We'll do everything we can to find out what happened to your sister."

Emily nodded, tears streaming down her face. "I just want justice for Sarah," she said.

Gurunadham stood up and placed a comforting hand on her shoulder. "We'll make sure we get it," he promised.

Detective Gurunadham sat across from Vimala, Sarah's best friend, in the small, cramped interview room. Vimala nervously twiddled her thumbs as she answered Gurunadham's questions.

"Can you tell me about your relationship with Sarah?" Gurunadham asked, his voice calm and steady.

"We were best friends," Vimala replied, her voice shaking. "We did everything together. We were inseparable."

"When was the last time you saw Sarah?"

"It was the night before she disappeared," Vimala said, her eyes filling with tears. "We had plans to go to the movies, but she had to cancel last minute. She said she had something important to do."

"Do you know what that something was?"

"No, she didn't tell me. But I knew she was going through some personal stuff at the time. She seemed really upset and distracted."

Gurunadham nodded, making a note in his notebook. "Did Sarah mention any problems or conflicts she was having with anyone? Family, friends, boyfriend?"

Vimala shook her head. "No, she didn't mention anything like that. She was just really preoccupied and upset."

"What about John Smith, Sarah's father's friend? Did she ever mention him to you?"

"No, I don't think so. I don't know who that is."

Gurunadham thanked Vimala for her time and let her leave. As he sat alone in the interview room, he couldn't shake off the feeling that something was off about John Smith. He made a mental note to look into him further in his investigation.

Detective Gurunadam had been investigating the unsolved case of Sarah for many years. He had interviewed Sarah's family members and friends, but had yet to find any solid evidence that would lead to the killer. However, during his latest round of interrogations, he had a suspicion that Sarah's father's friend, John Smith, could be the killer.

Gurunadam called John in for another round of questioning. John was visibly nervous and stuttered as he tried to answer Gurunadam's questions. "I swear, I had nothing to do with Sarah's murder," John pleaded. "I was at home with my family on the night of the murder, and I have several witnesses to back up my alibi."

Gurunadam asked John to provide the names of the witnesses, and John quickly supplied them. Gurunadam then interviewed the witnesses and found that their alibis matched John's story. He cross-checked the alibis with other evidence and found no discrepancies.

Gurunadam was disappointed that his suspicions about John had been proven false, but he was relieved that he now had solid evidence to rule John out as a suspect. He knew that he still had a long way to go in his investigation, but at least he could now focus on other leads.

Gurunadam still haunted by the unsolved case of Sarah, he knew that he couldn't give up until he found the killer and brought them to justice. He would not rest until he could provide closure for Sarah's family and finally lay his own haunted past to rest.

As Detective Gurunadam continued his investigation into the murder of Sarah, he began to focus on her classmates as potential suspects. One name that kept coming up in conversations with Sarah's friends and family was her math teacher, Satyamurthy. Gurunadam decided to pay him a visit to ask him a few questions.

When Gurunadam arrived at the school, he was greeted by Satyamurthy who seemed visibly uncomfortable and flustered. As Gurunadam began to ask him about his relationship with Sarah and whether he had noticed anything unusual leading up to her murder, Satyamurthy's discomfort increased. He kept fidgeting and avoiding eye contact, which only made Gurunadam more suspicious.

As the conversation continued, Satyamurthy's responses became increasingly evasive. He hesitated when answering questions and seemed to be hiding something. Gurunadam's instincts told him that Satyamurthy was not being truthful, and he made a mental note to look into the teacher's background more thoroughly.

Gurunadam's suspicions were further confirmed when he spoke with Sarah's classmates. They reported that Satyamurthy had been acting strange around Sarah in the weeks leading up to her murder and that he had made several inappropriate comments to her.

All of this evidence, combined with Satyamurthy's evasive behavior and discomfort during the interview, led Gurunadam to suspect that Satyamurthy may be the killer. He vowed to gather more solid evidence and build a case against him to bring justice to Sarah.

It is through further questioning of Satyamurthy that Gurunadam finally uncovers the truth behind Sarah's murder. The teacher reveals that he killed her because she had witnessed his affair with another teacher. The affair was the motive behind the crime. With this information, Gurunadam is able to arrest Satyamurthy and bring him to justice for Sarah's murder.

In the end, Gurunadam felt a sense of satisfaction and closure as he brought Sarah's killer to justice, but he also couldn't help but feel a sense of sadness for the young woman and her family who had to go through such a tragic event. He made a mental note to himself to always follow every lead and never give up until the truth is revealed.

Detective Gurunadam had finally found some rest after solving the Sarah murder case, but as he was watching the news, he saw a breaking story about the Andhra Pradesh Chief Minister being attacked in a public meeting. The case was now being handled by a special officer from the crime branch department, Ranjit. However, Gurunadam soon received a call asking for his help in investigating the attack on the AP CM.